This book belongs to:

....

....

To my family, for their love
and encouragement – AB

For Gracie – MB

Quarto is the authority on a wide range of topics.
Quarto educates, entertains and enriches the lives of
our readers—enthusiasts and lovers of hands-on living.
www.quartoknows.com

Author: Amanda Brandon
Illustrator: Mike Byrne
Designer: Victoria Kimonidou
Editor: Ellie Brough

© 2019 Quarto Publishing plc

This edition first published in 2019 by QED Publishing,
an imprint of The Quarto Group.
The Old Brewery, 6 Blundell Street,
London N7 9BH, United Kingdom.
T (0)20 7700 6700 F (0)20 7700 8066
www.QuartoKnows.com

A catalogue record for this book is available from the British Library.

ISBN 978 0 7112 5117 5

Manufactured in Shenzhen, China PP092019

9 8 7 6 5 4 3 2 1

UNICORN TRAINING

Amanda Brandon & Mike Byrne

Tilly Teasel loved to help at the
UNICORN RESCUE SANCTUARY.

She brushed the swishy tails of big unicorns
and polished the horns of little unicorns.

But what she really wanted,
was a unicorn of her own.

One day Splodge arrived at the Sanctuary.
He looked a little scruffy and a little sad. Tilly whistled.
He let out a PARP of sparkles. Dad sneezed.

"*I'll take him!*" Tilly said.

"Are you sure? He doesn't look well-trained to me," Dad said.

"I'll train him to be the best unicorn ever," Tilly said.

Splodge licked her.
Tilly felt fizzy and fuzzy inside.

Splodge loved his new home.
He loved the sofa...

...and especially
Tilly's snuggly bed.
Mum frowned:
*"I think he might
prefer the shed."*

That night Splodge whined and
cried, so Tilly sneaked him indoors.
"Don't worry, they'll soon love you
as much as I do," she whispered.

In the morning Splodge munched
two bowlfuls of moondrops and...

...Dad's slippers!

"Naughty Splodge!" Tilly hid the slippers.

She brushed his mane and polished his fur.
"You're the cleanest unicorn in the world now,"
Tilly said proudly.

He SWISHED
his sparkly tail...

CRASH

"Oops!" Tilly said.
"Let's go outside..."

Tilly studied her Unicorn Training Manual.
She told Splodge to sit and to roll over.

But Splodge
wouldn't listen.

She asked Splodge
to trot.

"WHOA!
Too fast!"

She threw down her manual.

"Unicorn Training is
IMPOSSIBLE!"

At home, Dad found his chewed-up
slippers. Mum held her broken vase.
"That unicorn is trouble!" Dad said.

Tilly wondered if they were right.
Unicorn training was harder
than she thought.

The next day Tilly tried to teach
Splodge just one thing – his name.

She called him. But
Splodge didn't respond.

Tilly held out a moondrop,
"Splodge!" she called.
He trotted to her.

She practised again and again until Splodge knew his name.

Mum tried calling Splodge to dinner. He gave her
a lick and tucked in. She felt fizzy and fuzzy inside.

Dad tried: *"Playtime, Splodge!"* Splodge bounded up to him.
He gave him a lick. Dad felt fizzy and fuzzy inside.

Soon Splodge learned to sit, shake
hands and roll over. He even learned
how to take Tilly for a ride.

Splodge was a
STAR PUPIL!

Tilly was so proud of Splodge.
Mum and Dad were proud of Tilly.

"He's the best unicorn ever!"
Tilly said. They all hugged Splodge.

He felt

FIZZY

and

FUZZY

inside.

NEXT STEPS

Discussion and comprehension

Discuss the story with the children and ask the following questions, encouraging them to take turns and give full answers if they are able to. Offer support by turning to the appropriate pages of the book if needed.

- What exactly is a unicorn? What other animal is a unicorn like?
- Tell me about the ways that Tilly persevered with the training.
- What do you understand by being responsible? In what ways have you been responsible?
- What made Tilly say that unicorn training was IMPOSSIBLE!?

Top Ten Tips

Give each child a piece of paper folded in half with *Tilly's Top Unicorn Tips* (included below) printed on one side of the paper. Read through these with the children, asking if they think they offer good advice for being responsible for a pet. Ask the children to think of a pet that they would like to have and write its name on the top of the other half of the paper. Ask the children to write five tips for looking after their pet. Allow the children to share the name of their pet, and their tips for being responsible for them.

The Letter 'U' is for Unicorn.

Give each child an A4 piece of brightly coloured sugar paper with a large letter U in different coloured paper stuck on to it. Give the children felt tip pens and ask them to make the top left of the U into the unicorn's head with an eye and a smiley mouth. Ask them to draw on a unicorn's horn, a long mane and a long tail. When they have finished, they can write at the bottom 'U is for Unicorn'.

☆ Tilly's Top Unicorn Tips ☆

1. Reward good behaviour with moondrops.
2. Polish fur daily with foamy flutter bubbles.
3. Keep snug with a double quilted unicorn duvet.
4. Buy Dad a supersize poop scoop.
5. Support your local rescue sanctuary.